A Haights Cross Communications ⟶ Company

Published by
Sundance Publishing
P.O. Box 1326
234 Taylor Street
Littleton, MA 01460
800-343-8204
www.sundancepub.com

First published 1999 by
Edizioni EL
Via J. Ressel, 5
34147 San Dorligo della Valle (TS)
Italy

Exclusive North American Distribution: Sundance Publishing

ISBN 0-7608-6735-6

Printed in Canada

Super Cat to the Rescue

Agostino Traini

sundance
A Haights Cross Communications Company

Miceville used to be a nice place to live. That was before five mean cats moved in to the next town. Then all of the mice were afraid—except for Victor.

Victor had a plan. He was going to build a big mechanical cat. "Super Cat and I will protect Miceville," Victor told everyone.

The other mice wanted to believe Victor. But they didn't.

Some mice even laughed at him.

"Victor's plan will never work," they told each other.

Victor worked day after day on Super Cat. Building a giant mechanical cat was hard work.

When everything was done, Victor painted Super Cat yellow. Then he gave him two eyes, two sharp teeth, and some whiskers.

Victor didn't know that the mean cats had already attacked Miceville. Mice were running here, there, and everywhere.

"Run for your lives!" they yelled. "The cats are coming! The cats are coming!"

In all the excitement, little Binky Mouse was left alone in the park. Soon the mean cats found her.

"Yum," said the biggest cat.

All of the cats licked their lips.

"Oh no," yelled a mouse.
"They've got Binky!"

The mice ran to Victor's house. "We have to save little Binky!" they screamed.

Victor knew just what to do. "This is a job for Super Cat," he said. He jumped inside Super Cat and roared off to the park.

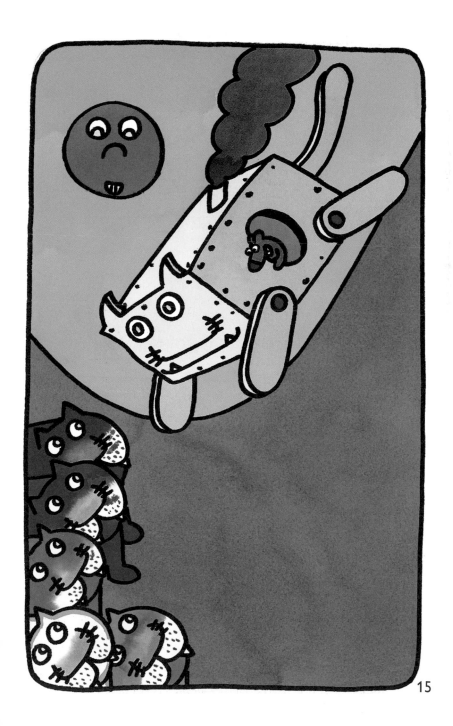

Super Cat got to the park just in time. The mean cats were so surprised, they forgot all about little Binky.

They had never seen a cat like Super Cat. They fought him long and hard.

Finally, the mean cats gave up and ran away. Victor climbed out of Super Cat. Little Binky Mouse was safe. But Super Cat looked terrible.

"Oh no," said Victor. "Super Cat is broken."

It was getting late. Victor decided to take Binky home and come back later to fix Super Cat.

Everyone thanked Victor for saving Binky.

"I'm going home to get my tools," said Victor. "Super Cat is broken."

It was late when Victor got home. He was so tired, he fell asleep. The other mice came by to see if Victor needed help fixing Super Cat.

They decided to surprise Victor
by fixing Super Cat themselves.
That was how they could thank
him for saving Binky.

The mice worked all night.
They fixed Super Cat's dents.
Then they painted him red.

The next day, Victor went to fix Super Cat.

"Wow, you look brand new!" said Victor. "Who did this?"

"We did," said the mice as they arrived at the park. "We're sorry we laughed at you. Your plan was a good one."

"That's OK," said Victor.

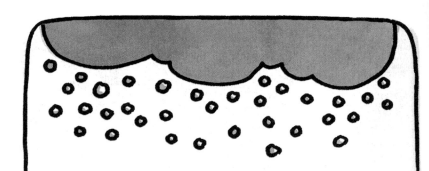

Then Victor took his friends for a ride up into the mountains. Now that Miceville was safe from the five mean cats, there was plenty of time to have fun.

Hooray for Super Cat!

Victor is thinking about a key for
Super Cat. Which of these five
keys matches his idea?

28

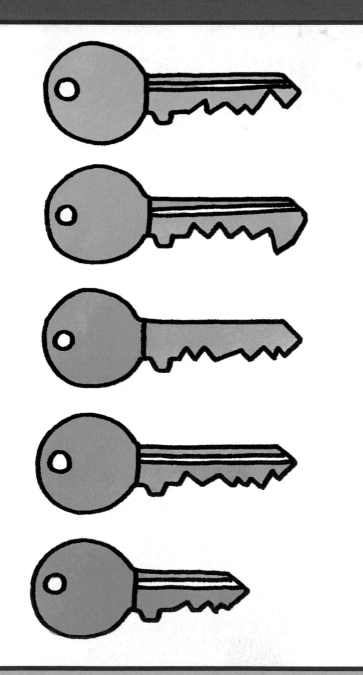

Can you find Victor?
He's holding a wrench.

SunLit Library

SET 1	SET 2
Anita the Tree	Alexander the Bat
Daisy and Tina	The Captain and the Whale
The Giraffe Family Vacation	Granny Vanilla Takes to the Sky
Granny Vanilla's Magic Cookies	Holly the Hoozeewhat
Moka All Year Round	Katy and the Telephone
Moka Delivers the Mail	The Lily Pad Olympics
Mole and Mouse	The Long Bus Ride
Mr. Kite Gets Stuck	Moka Above the Clouds
Nikki's Costume Party	Nikki and the Ark
A New Friend	Pedro the Painter
Scout Flies Away	Summer Adventure
Sunny's Red Spots	**Super Cat to the Rescue**